FREDDIE & GINGERSNAP

Vincent X. Kirsch

Disney · HYPERION BOOKS

NEW YORK

To a little dinosaur like Freddie, it looked as if
the other dinosaurs had their heads in the clouds.
"What's that like?" he wondered.
He went to find out.

For a little dragon named Gingersnap, it looked as if
flying would be the easiest thing to do.
"Could I fly?" she asked herself.

So she tried.

You might say that was the luckiest day of their lives,
except dinosaurs and dragons stayed as far away from each other as possible.

Freddie and Gingersnap stood
nose to nose
and toes to toes.

They stared eye to eye.
They scowled and they growled.

They clicked the pointed claws on their fingers—

Freddie howled.

And Gingersnap stomped.

Freddie stomped.

STOMP! STOMP!

And Gingersnap howled.

HOOOWL!

They stomped
and they howled
at the same time.

HOOOWL!
STOMP! STOMP!
STOMP!
STOMP!
HOOOWL!

Gingersnap chased Freddie, and . . .

she caught him.

"I saw what you did!" said Freddie.
He wiggled free.
"But you'll never catch me!" said Gingersnap.

Freddie chased Gingersnap . . .

and he caught her just in time.

He held on very tight.
"Don't worry!" said Freddie. "I won't let go!"

And . . .

PLIP!

PLOP!

he didn't.

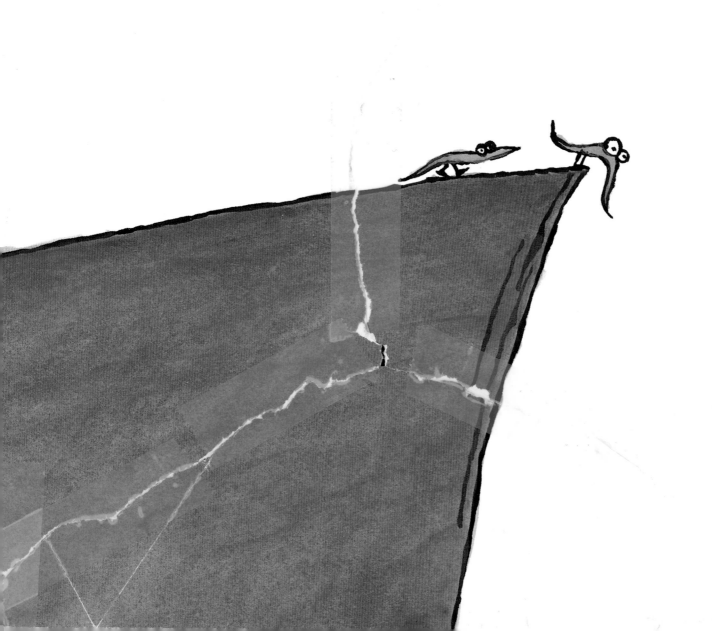

Freddie and Gingersnap ended up among the thistles and thorns.
They knew they could not stay there forever.

"Do you know what clouds are like?" Freddie asked.
"I could introduce you," Gingersnap answered, "if I knew how to fly."

"Well, I know how to fly," said Freddie.
"I learned the trick from you!"
This was quite a surprise to Gingersnap!

Freddie started to jump higher and higher, as high as he could.
Gingersnap jumped higher and higher, just as high.

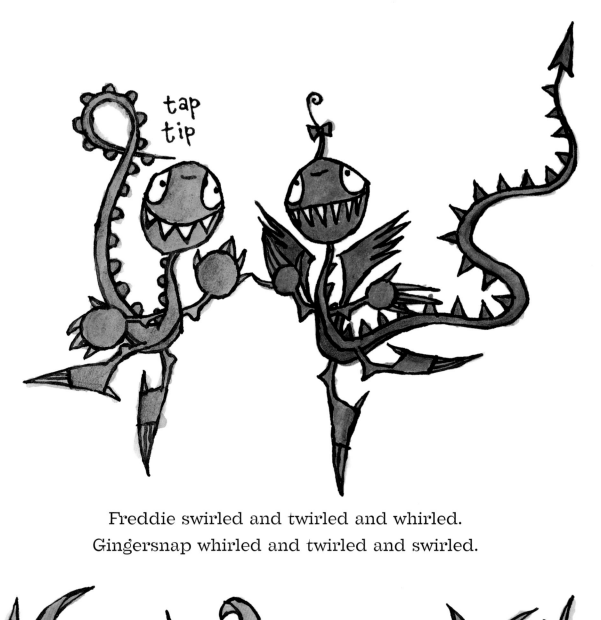

tap
tip

Freddie swirled and twirled and whirled.
Gingersnap whirled and twirled and swirled.

tap
tip

Freddie flap-flapped his arms.
Up, up, up he went.

Gingersnap flap-flapped hers.
Up, up, up she went, right behind him.

"You definitely don't know how to fly," Gingersnap observed.
"But you do!" said Freddie.
"Just do exactly what I do!"

Freddie tapped the tip of his tail to his nose two times.

tap
tip

Gingersnap tapped the tip of her tail to her nose two times . . .

and it *was* the easiest thing to do.

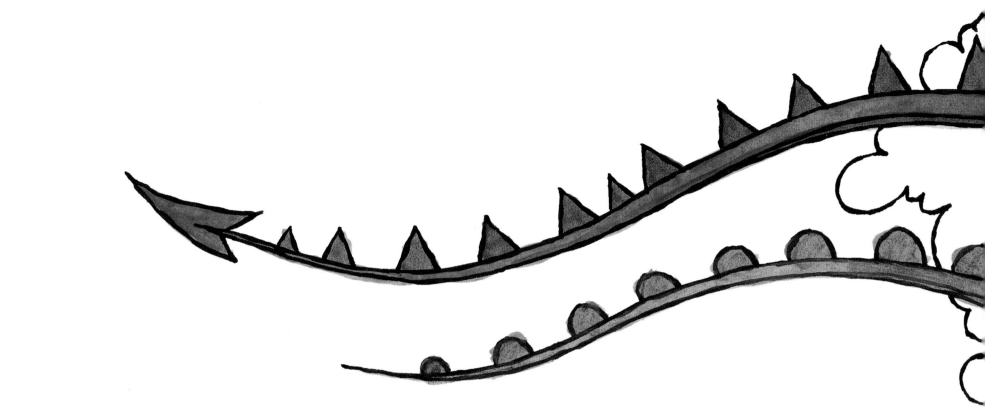

Gingersnap reached out and grabbed hold of Freddie.

She held on very tight.
"Don't worry," she said. "I won't let go!"

And she didn't.

You can certainly say that it was the luckiest day in
Freddie's and Gingersnap's lives.

At least, so far.

Printed in Malaysia
First Edition
1 3 5 7 9 10 8 6 4 2
H106-9333-5-13244

Library of Congress Cataloging-in-Publication Data

Kirsch, Vincent X., author, illustrator.
   Freddie & Gingersnap / by Vincent X. Kirsch.—First edition.
       pages cm
   Summary: Dinosaurs and dragons rarely get along, but when Freddie, a little dinosaur with his head in the clouds, meets Gingersnap, a little dragon trying to learn to fly, they soon find common ground.
   ISBN 978-1-4231-5958-2 (alk. paper)
[1. Friendship—Fiction. 2. Dinosaurs—Fiction. 3. Dragons—Fiction.] I. Title. II. Title: Freddie and Gingersnap.
   PZ7.K6383Fre 2013
   [E]—dc23   2012048390.

Text is set in Farao
Designed by Tanya Ross-Hughes
Reinforced binding

Visit www.disneyhyperionbooks.com